The Mess Detectives
Case #578:
Dial M for Mercy

Written by Doug Peterson
Illustrated by Ron Eddy & John Trent

BIG IDEA
BOOKS®

Zonderkidz

BIG IDEA BOOKS

www.bigidea.com

Zonder**kidz**.

The children's group of Zondervan
www.zonderkidz.com

The Mess Detectives: Case # 578-Dial M for Mercy
Copyright © 2005 by Big Idea, Inc.
Illustrations copyright © 2005 by Big Idea, Inc.
Requests for information should be addressed to:
Zonderkidz, Grand Rapids, Michigan 49530

Library of Congress Cataloging-in-Publication Data

Peterson, Doug.
 Dial M for mercy / by Doug Peterson.
   p. cm.
 Summary: Detective Larry the Cucumber and Bob the Tomato teach Percy Pea about forgiveness.
 ISBN 0-310-70740-4 (hardcover)
 [1. Christian life--Fiction. 2. Forgiveness--Fiction. 3. Vegetables--Fiction.] I. Title.
 PZ7.P44334Di 2005
 [E]--dc22

                                                                        2004012271

Written by: Doug Peterson
Editor: Cindy Kenney
Illustrations and Design: Big Idea Design
Art Direction: John Trent

Printed in China
05 06 07 08/LPC/5 4 3 2 1

FILE NEXT WEEK

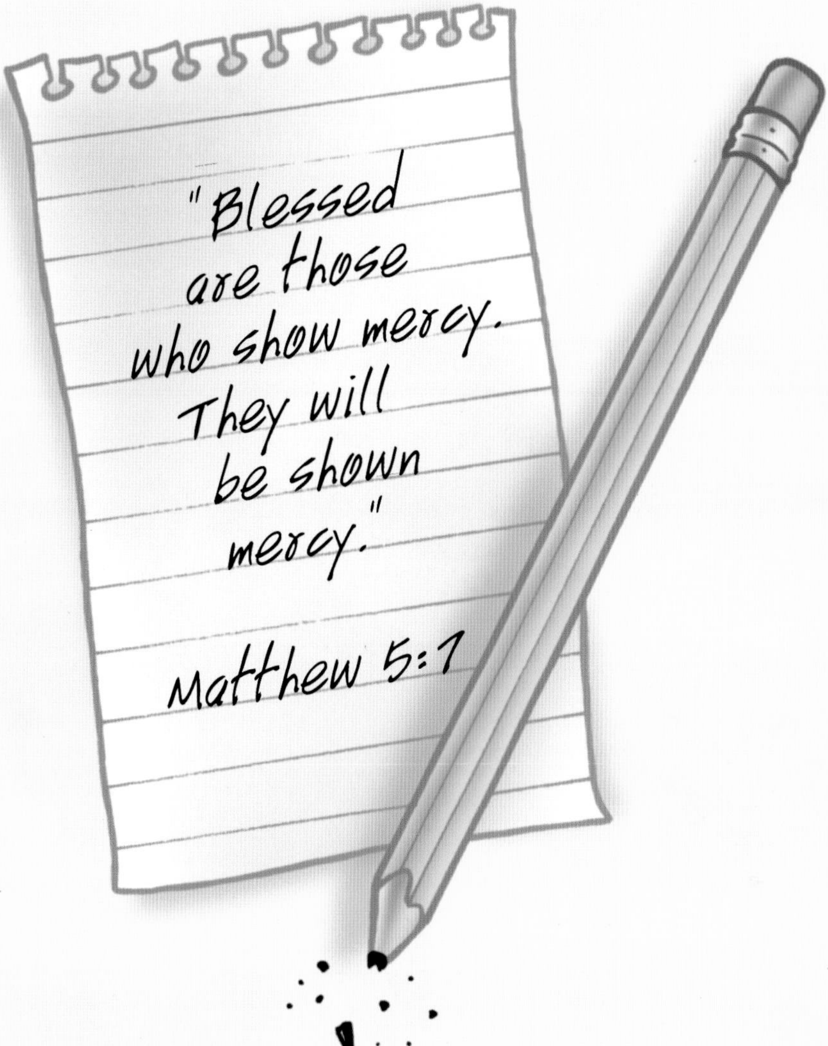

Ladies and gentlemen, the story you are about to read is silly. The names have been changed to protect the serious.

This is our city—a city of messes. Our job is to get people out of them. We are the Mess Detectives.

My name is Detective Larry the Cucumber, and my partner is Bob the Tomato. He carries a badge. I carry a badger.

Don't ask why.

10:06 a.m.

Bob and I were working the
Mess Watch when we got a phone call
on our "mess-line." The mess-line was
something new. If people were in a mess,
they simply dialed M on their telephones
to reach us right away.

BRRINNGGG!

"This is the mess-line," I said.

"Do you have any monkeys for sale?" asked the person on the phone.

Monkeys? Something was wrong. I could sense it.

"Sorry, wrong number," I snapped. "We handle messes, not monkeys." I slammed down the phone.

I was mad because our mess-line was messing up. For some strange reason, people had been dialing M for monkeys, instead M for messes. They had a lot of nerve.

10:30 a.m.

While riding around in our police car, we spotted Percy Pea dragging a huge load of newspapers.

"My name is Detective Larry, and this is my partner Bob," I told Percy as I took out my notebook. "Bob carries a badge. I carry a badger. Don't ask why."

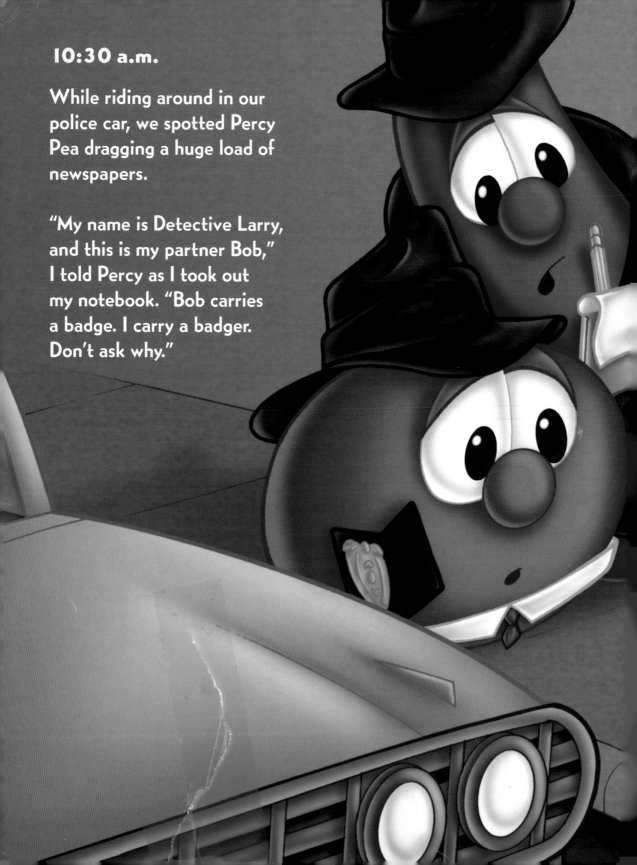

"What seems to be the problem?" asked Bob.

Percy sighed. "I delivered Laura's newspapers today," he said. "But I lost five dollars of her delivery tips. She's gonna be mad!"

"How did it happen?" Bob asked.

"I have a hole in my pocket," Percy said.

"Did you know that?"

Percy looked away. "Yeah, I knew. My mom told me to wear different pants today, so she could fix the hole. But...I really like these pants, so I wore them anyway."

I could see why he wanted to wear them. They were spiffy pants.

10:36 a.m.

Laura Carrot came strolling down the sidewalk, straight for us. If she found out that Percy had lost her newspaper money, things could get ugly.

"Run for it!" I shouted to Percy.

"No! Don't run," Bob corrected, rolling his eyes. "Listen, Percy. Everyone messes up sometimes. If you tell Laura what happened and say you're sorry, she might have mercy on you."

"Mercy?" Percy asked. "What's that?"

"Mercy is when someone gives you a second chance after you've messed up," Bob said. "God wants us to show mercy, Percy."

"You can be Mercy Percy," I laughed. "That's funny." I made a note of that. Bob just rolled his eyes.

I couldn't believe it. When Percy told Laura what had happened, she was really disappointed, but she didn't get mad.

"Mistakes happen, so don't worry about it," she said to Percy. "But I'd get that pocket fixed if I were you."

Laura forgave him! She showed mercy.

I started to make a note of that when my pencil broke.

"Drat. Can you sharpen this?" I asked my badger.

My badger sharpened the pencil with his
teeth as we drove back to headquarters.
It looked like the case was closed.

Or so we thought.

1:05 p.m.

We were eating sundaes when we got another call on the mess-line.

"Mess Detectives here," I answered.

"I would like an order of meatloaf," said the person on the other end.

Meatloaf? The mess-line was messing up again.

"You're supposed to dial M for messes, not for meatloaf!" I yelled into the phone. I felt like dialing M for mad.

1:10 p.m.

While driving up and down the city streets, we passed a lemonade stand and spotted Junior Asparagus. He looked upset, so we stopped to find out why.

"Anything wrong?" asked Bob.

"There sure is," Junior muttered. "I was helping Percy Pea with his lemonade stand today when I set a dollar on the table and the wind blew it away. I lost Percy's money!"

"Didn't Percy have a box for the money?" Bob asked.

"Well…yeah," said Junior. "That's why I feel so bad. Percy told me not to put the money on the table. But I didn't think anything would happen."

Junior had messed up big time. "Don't worry, Percy will understand," I explained. "Laura showed mercy to Percy. So I'm sure Percy will have mercy on you. Mercy Percy! Get it?"

I really cracked myself up.

"That's just it. When I told Percy what I did," Junior sobbed, "he was so mad! He said I had to work at his lemonade stand all week— without getting paid!"

I was shocked. To top it off, my pencil broke again. I looked to my badger for help.

2:30 p.m.

Bob and I drove through Bumblyburg, looking for Percy. We needed to pick him up for questioning.

As we pulled into the donut shop parking lot, our car phone rang.

"Mess-line," I answered.

"I'd like a malt, two mousetraps, and a marimba," said the person on the other end.

I slammed down the phone. Someone had really messed up! People were dialing M for malts, mousetraps, marimbas, meatloaf, and monkeys!

I made a note of that. Then I made a note of how mad I was getting when my pencil point broke again, and guess what happened.

You got it. My badger sharpened it.

That's when we spotted Percy. He was on the run.

We tore out of the parking lot and flew around the corner. Bob's face smooshed up against the window as I pulled the police car to the curb, tires screeching. Bob and I leaped out of the car and blocked Percy's path.

"Stop! In the name of messes!" Bob shouted, showing his badge.

I showed my badger.

My badger growled, and Percy came to a sudden stop. He was out of breath.

"Why are you running?" Bob asked.

"I'm trying to get away from Laura," Percy gasped. "Laura said I had to pay her the money I lost after all. But this morning she said she wasn't even mad."

"Why do you think she changed her mind?" Bob asked.

That was a good question.

"I don't know, but I have to go," Percy sputtered.

"Are you sure you don't know why she changed her mind?" Bob asked.

Percy looked around, afraid that Laura was right behind him. "I...I guess she talked to Junior Asparagus."

"Why did she change her mind after talking to Junior?" Bob continued.

I had no idea where Bob was going with this.

"Well…" Percy looked Bob straight in the eyes. "Maybe she was mad when she found out about Junior."

"What about Junior?"

Bob would not let up.

"She probably heard Junior lost my money."

"That's right," Bob confirmed. "And what did you do?"

I was still clueless.

"I got really mad," Percy confessed.

"Yet Laura showed you mercy when you lost her money," Bob reminded him.

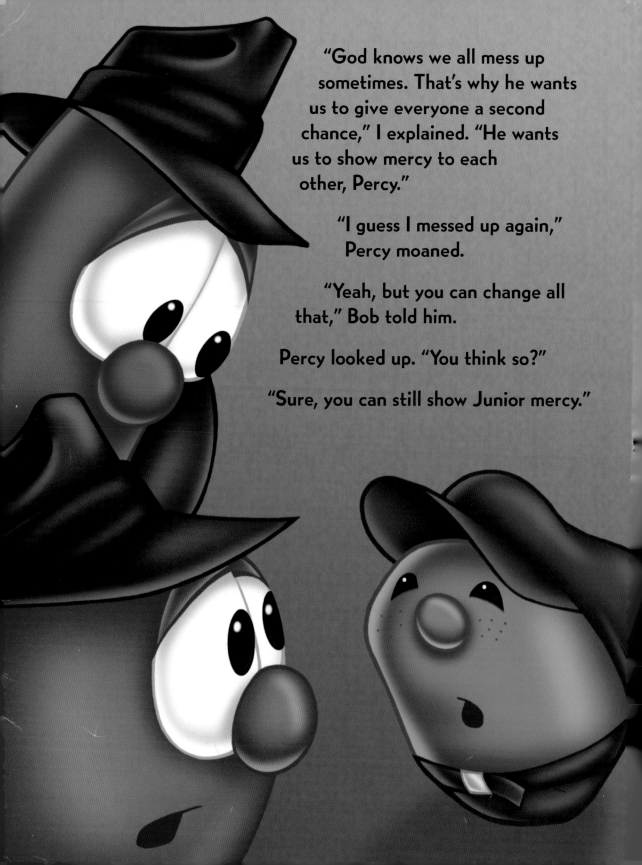

"God knows we all mess up sometimes. That's why he wants us to give everyone a second chance," I explained. "He wants us to show mercy to each other, Percy."

"I guess I messed up again," Percy moaned.

"Yeah, but you can change all that," Bob told him.

Percy looked up. "You think so?"

"Sure, you can still show Junior mercy."

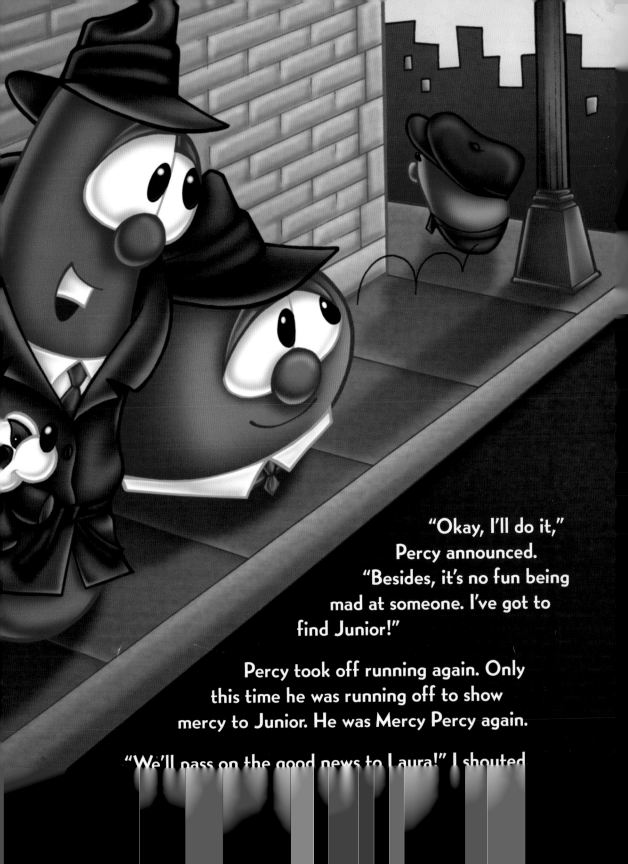

"Okay, I'll do it,"
Percy announced.
"Besides, it's no fun being
mad at someone. I've got to
find Junior!"

Percy took off running again. Only
this time he was running off to show
mercy to Junior. He was Mercy Percy again.

"We'll pass on the good news to Laura!" I shouted

3:04 p.m.

Another day, another mess solved. Bob and I hopped back into our car when the mess-line rang again.

"What is it this time?" I muttered, picking up my phone.

"Hi, Detective Larry," said the person on the phone. "This is Marvin the Phone Guy. I just wanted to let you know that the mess-line has been messed up today."

"Yeah, I noticed!"

"I'm sorry," said Marvin.
"I made a few mistakes, but I'm working on the problem."

I wanted to yell at Marvin the Phone Guy. I wanted to tell
him he messed up my day, and that he better fix the mess-line
pronto, or else. But that's when something interesting happened.

My badger handed me my sharpened pencil. As I stared at my pencil, I remembered we all make mistakes. I broke my pencil more than one time today, but my badger didn't get mad, even though he warned me not to press so hard.

My badger had sharpened my pencil every time without complaining—without even badgering me about it.

Percy was right. It's no fun being mad. Besides, Marvin
was fixing the mess-line.

"That's okay," I said to Marvin. "We all mess up sometimes."

3:07 p.m.

"Who was that?" Bob asked. "Wrong number again?"

"No, it was Marvin the Phone Guy," I said. "He dialed M for mercy, and that's what he got."

Dialing M for mercy was definitely the right number.

To learn more about mercy, read the Parable of the Unmerciful Servant. Check out Matthew 18:21–35.